t tell lise about cro t nat s
I must not tell lise about croco not lose my gloves
I must not tell lise about crocodiles and I must not lose my gloves
I must not tell lise about crocodiles and I must not lose my gloves
must not tell lise about crocodiles and I must not lose my gloves
must not tell lise about crocodiles and I must not lose my gloves
must not tell lise about crocodiles and I must not lose my gloves
must not tell lise about crocodiles and I must not lose my gloves
must not tell lise about crocodiles and I must not lose my gloves
must not tell lise about crocodiles and I must not lose my gloves
must not tell lise about crocodiles and I must not lose my gloves
must not tell lise about crocodiles and I must not lose my glove
must not tell lise about crocodiles and I must not lose my gloves
must not tell lise about crocodiles and I must not lose my gloves
must not tell lise about crocodiles and I must not lose my gloves
I must not tell lise about crocodiles and I must not lose my gloves
I must not tell lise about crocodiles and I must not lose my glove
I must not tell lise about crocodiles and I must not lose my glove
I must not tell lise about crocodiles and I must not lose my gloves
I must not tell lise about croodiles and I must not dose my gloves
must not tell lise about crocodiles and I must not lose my gloves
I must not tell lise about crocodiles and I must not lose my gloves
I must not tell lise about crocodiles and I must not lose my glove
I must not tell lise about crocodiles and I must not lose my gloves
I must not tell lise about crocodiles and I must not lose my gloves

John Patrick Norman McHennessy-the boy who was always late

JOHN BURNINGHAM

ALFRED A. KNOPF ![horse] NEW YORK

THIS IS A BORZOI BOOK PUBLISHED BY ALFRED A. KNOPF

Copyright © 1987 by John Burningham

All rights reserved. Published in the United States by Alfred A. Knopf, an imprint of Random House Children's Books, a division of Random House, Inc., New York. Originally published by Crown Publishers, Inc., in 1987.

Knopf, Borzoi Books, and the colophon are registered trademarks of Random House, Inc.

Visit us on the Web! www.randomhouse.com/kids

Educators and librarians, for a variety of teaching tools, visit us at www.randomhouse.com/teachers

The Library of Congress has cataloged the original edition of this work as follows:
Burningham, John.
John Patrick Norman McHennessy: the boy who was always late.
Summary: A teacher regrets his decision to disbelieve a student's outlandish excuses for being tardy.
[1. Tardiness—Fiction. 2. Excuses—Fiction. 3. Schools—Fiction.] I. Title.
PZ7.B936Jo 1988
[E]
87-20165

ISBN 978-0-375-85220-6 (trade) — ISBN 978-0-375-95220-3 (lib. bdg.)

MANUFACTURED IN MALAYSIA
July 2008
10 9 8 7 6 5 4 3 2 1

John Patrick Norman McHennessy set off
along the road to learn.

On the way a crocodile came out of a drain and got hold of his satchel.

John Patrick Norman McHennessy pulled and pulled but the crocodile would not let go.

He threw a glove into the air and the crocodile snapped at the glove and let go of the satchel.

John Patrick Norman McHennessy hurried along the road to learn but the crocodile had made him late.

"John Patrick Norman McHennessy, you are late and where is your other glove?"

"I am late, Sir, because on the way a crocodile came out of a drain and got hold of my satchel, and would only let go when I threw my glove, which he ate."

"There are no crocodiles living in the drains around here. You are to stay in late and write out 300 times, 'I must not tell lies about crocodiles and I must not lose my glove.'"

So John Patrick Norman McHennessy stayed in late and wrote out 300 times, "I must not tell lies about crocodiles and I must not lose my glove."

John Patrick Norman McHennessy hurried off
along the road to learn.

But on the way a lion came out of the bushes
and tore his trousers.

He managed to climb up a tree. He stayed up the tree until the lion lost interest in him and went away.

John Patrick Norman McHennessy hurried off along the road to learn but he was late because of the lion.

"You are late again, John Patrick Norman McHennessy, and you have torn your trousers."

"I am late, Sir, because on my way here a lion jumped out of the bushes and tore my trousers and I had to climb a tree and wait until the lion went away."

"There are no such things as lions in the bushes around here. You are to stand in the corner and say out loud 400 times, 'I must not tell lies about lions and I must not tear my trousers.'"

John Patrick Norman McHennessy stood in the
corner and said out loud 400 times, "I must not
tell lies about lions and I must not tear my
trousers."

John Patrick Norman McHennessy hurried off
along the road to learn.

But on the way, as he was crossing the bridge
over the river, a huge tidal wave swept him off his feet.

He managed to cling on to the rail until the wave had passed and the water had gone down.

John Patrick Norman McHennessy hurried along the road to learn but he was late because of the tidal wave.

"You are late again, John Patrick Norman McHennessy, and your clothes are wet."

"I am late, Sir, because on my way here, as I was crossing the bridge, a tidal wave swept me off my feet and made me wet and I had to cling on to the rail until the water went down."

"There are no such things as tidal waves in the rivers around here that sweep people off the bridges. You will be locked in until you have written down 500 times, 'I must not tell lies about tidal waves in the river and I must not get my clothes wet.' And if you keep telling these lies and being late I may have to hit you with my stick."

So John Patrick Norman McHennessy was locked in until he had written down 500 times, "I must not tell lies about tidal waves in the river and I must not get my clothes wet."

John Patrick Norman McHennessy hurried
along the road to learn.

On the way nothing happened and he was able
to be on time.

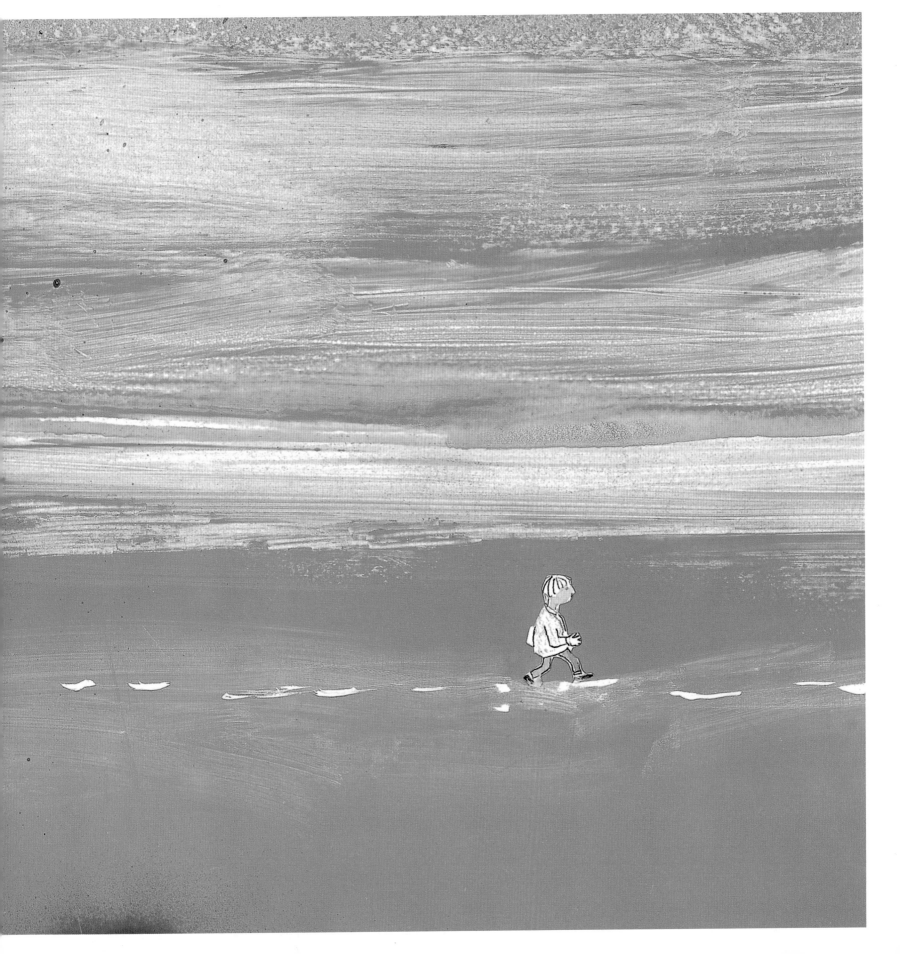

"John Patrick Norman McHennessy, I am being held up in the roof by a great big hairy gorilla. You are to get me down at once."

"There are no such things as great big hairy gorillas in the roofs around here, Sir."

And John Patrick Norman McHennessy set off
along the road to learn.